First published in the United States
of America in 1990 by The Mallard Press

Mallard Press and its accompanying design
and logo are trademarks of BDD Promotional
Book Company, Inc.

Produced by
Twin Books
15 Sherwood Place
Greenwich, CT 06830

ISBN 0 792 45401 4

Printed in Hong Kong

Disney's

MICKEY MOUSE

IN

SKY ISLAND

Written by
Nikki Grimes

TWIN BOOKS

MALLARD
PRESS

High above the Chockridge Mountains flew a small aircraft with Mickey Mouse at the controls and Goofy in the passenger seat. Mickey was giving Goofy his first flying lesson.

"What do you think of flying, Goofy?" asked Mickey.

"Gawrsh," said Goofy, "we're awful high, Mick."

Mickey laughed. "Don't worry, Goofy, we won't fall. Did you bring your camera?"

"I sure did, Mick," said Goofy. "I've got my camera right here," he added, patting his pocket.

"Good," said Mickey. "You'll get great pictures from up here."

"You mean like that?" said Goofy, staring at a man who was waving at them.

Mickey followed Goofy's gaze. There was, indeed, a man waving at them from a strange-looking aircraft. As they drew closer, Mickey rubbed his eyes. He couldn't believe what he saw.

"That car's flying, and it doesn't even have wings!" said Goofy.

"Well, I'll be!" said Mickey. "Come on! Let's follow him!" Mickey's plane flew faster and faster, but just as they were about to catch up with the flying car, it flew into a cloud.

Mickey flew around the cloud, and waited for the car to fly out on the other side. But it never did.

"Hey!" said Mickey, puzzled. "Where did it go?"

Mickey flew into the cloud to look for the flying car, but found nothing. Disappointed, he and Goofy returned to the airport.

As soon as the plane touched down, Mickey found Captain Doberman and told him what they had seen.

"Did you bump your head while you were up there?" chuckled the captain.

"I tell you, I saw it with my own eyes!" insisted Mickey.

"I took a picture of it with my pocket camera," said Goofy. "Would that help?"

Doberman had the film developed right away. When he saw the photo, he knew Mickey hadn't been imagining things.

An hour later, Mickey and Captain Doberman took off. The captain wanted to see the flying car with his own eyes.

They flew around for quite a while, but saw nothing. They were about to give up and go back to the airport when the car Mickey had seen flew out of a cloud. The same man was driving it.

"There he is again!" cried Mickey, pointing.

They tried to follow him, but suddenly their plane couldn't move!

"I guess we're stuck until he lets us go, Mickey," said the captain. "But keep your motor running."

Moments later, Mickey's plane zoomed forward and they were free. But the flying car was long gone.

Back at the airport, Mickey refueled his plane again. "I'm going to find that guy," he told Captain Doberman. "Now I'm really curious."

"Be careful, Mickey," cautioned the captain. "If that man can make a car fly, there's no telling what else he can do."

Mickey and Goofy took off. Goofy was watching the sky, while Mickey was looking down. He thought the man might be hiding in the mountains below.

"Hey, Mickey," said Goofy, "maybe we'd better go back. It looks like it's going to rain soon. See? There's a black rain cloud!"

Mickey looked up and saw the cloud. Somehow, it didn't look like a plain old rain cloud. Mickey flew closer to investigate.

Mickey flew into the dark grey cloud. "I must be going crazy!" he said. He couldn't believe what he saw. The rain cloud hid a huge chunk of earth, suspended right in the middle of the sky. Thick tree roots hung down from it.

"Wow!" said Goofy. "Let's look at the top, Mick!"

The top of the island in the sky was a wonderful city.

"I don't believe it!" said Mickey.

"Neither do I," said Goofy. "Let's go home and forget the whole thing." But Mickey went down for a better look.

A man stood on the balcony of the tallest building. "Well, now that you've found me," he said, "come on down."

The man went inside the building, then quickly returned. Without warning, Mickey's plane stopped in midair.

"Don't worry," said the man. "Your plane is safe. Just climb over the side and walk down."

Cautiously, Mickey and Goofy got out and walked down an invisible ramp.

"Welcome to Sky Island," said the man. "I'm Dr. Future."

Mickey introduced himself and Goofy, then questioned the scientist about the flying car and the island in the sky.

"The answer is simple," said Dr. Future. "Let me show you." He took them to his laboratory.

"What's that?" Mickey pointed to something that looked like a hair dryer. Dr. Future picked it up and aimed it at Goofy, who rose from the floor. Future then lowered Goofy back down. Mickey was amazed.

"It's my portable floater gun," said Dr. Future, grinning playfully. "I have learned how to control gravity."

"Gosh, Dr. Future," said Mickey. "A lot of people would be interested in your invention! Are you going to sell it?"

The doctor smiled. "I don't need any money, and I'm afraid that some men might use it for evil."

"But, Doctor—"

"Sorry, Mickey," said the doctor. "My mind is made up. Now, would you boys like to take a ride in my autoplane?"

"Would we ever!" said Mickey, excited.

Soon they were soaring over Sky Island. When they turned around, another plane came into view. The pilot was someone Mickey and Goofy knew well—Bad Pete.

"Hiya, Doc!" Pete called from his plane. "Can I visit your island?"

"Don't let him, Dr. Future!" cried Mickey. "He's a criminal!"

"Oh, no," said Pete sweetly. "I used to be bad, but I've changed."

Dr. Future believed Pete, and invited him to Sky Island.

Back at his house, Dr. Future raised his glass of lemonade in a toast to Pete. "To a bad man gone good," he said.

"Pete sure seems different," Goofy whispered to Mickey. "Not mean and nasty anymore. What could have changed him?"

But Mickey didn't think Pete had really changed.

Suddenly, as Goofy leaned against the wall, something opened out from it and knocked him flat. It was the heavy metal door of a safe.

"Hey! What do we have here?" said Pete, always interested in something like a safe.

"Sorry!" said Dr. Future. "That safe opens automatically every night at this time. I check on my plans once a day."

"Plans?" asked Pete. "What kind of plans?"

"Oh, for the things I've invented, like my floater gun," Dr. Future explained.

The doctor quickly glanced at the papers in his safe and closed it. Mickey saw Pete glance at his watch. It was nine o'clock. *You shouldn't have told him that, Dr. Future,* he thought to himself.

The next day, Mickey, Goofy and Pete toured Sky Island. Pete behaved like a model citizen. But that evening, about 8:15, he dropped his nice-guy act.

Pete pulled a gun, forced Mickey, Goofy and Dr. Future into an upstairs room, and tied them up. "You sure fell for my act," he sneered, pulling the ropes tight. "I gotta hand it to you, Doc—I can sure use that floater gun. It'll come in handy for stealin' heavy stuff like gold!" Pete went downstairs to wait for the safe to open.

Mickey tried to wiggle out of the ropes, but it was no use. "Doctor, what can we do?" he asked. "We've got to stop Pete!"

The scientist wasn't worried. He explained that unless he entered a special program in his main computer by 8:30 every night, the island would fall back to earth.

"But, Doctor," cried Mickey, alarmed, "we'll fall, too!"

"Yes. But at least Pete won't get his hands on my floater gun."

Mickey didn't want to give up without a fight. "Tell me how to program your computer," he said. "I'll try to get to it in time."

"If I do, you must promise me to stop Pete before you program the computer."

Mickey promised, and Dr. Future gave him the secret program. Then, still tied up, Mickey bounced the chair steadily toward the door. Soon he bounced himself out of the room.

Mickey bounced through the door to the roof, and over to the edge. The ground seemed a long way down. Just then, he saw Pete below. Mickey knew it was his only chance. Chair and all, he threw himself off the roof and luckily landed directly on Pete. The fall broke Mickey's chair and loosened his ropes—not a minute too soon. When Pete came to, he started swinging!

Mickey teased Pete, saying, "Come and get me!" He ran for the lab, with Pete in pursuit. Mickey waited behind the lab door, then swung around and thumped Pete on the head with his fist. Pete fell to the floor, dazed.

But that only stopped him for a second. Mickey grabbed the floater gun. It lifted Pete off the floor, made him hit his head against the ceiling and knocked him out.

Then Mickey looked at the clock. "Oh, no!" he cried. "It's too late!"

Hoping the clock was fast, Mickey quickly programmed the computer.

Upstairs, Goofy and Dr. Future held their breath as they felt the island begin to fall. "I guess Mickey didn't succeed," said the doctor. "At least my floater gun is safe!"

Suddenly, they stopped falling.

"What happened?" said Dr. Future. Then they heard someone at the door. It was Mickey!

"Well," said Mickey, untying his friends, "I did it!"

They raced to the lab, where Dr. Future used the floater gun to put Pete back in his plane.

He told Pete to put on his parachute, then sent Pete's plane miles from the island. When Dr. Future turned off the floater gun, the plane started falling.

The doctor then called Captain Doberman and invited him to Sky Island. He had something to tell all of them.

After Captain Doberman arrived, Dr. Future turned to Mickey. "You saved my island and my floater gun," he said, "and I'm very grateful. But I'm afraid I must go away, so my invention will never fall into the hands of criminals like Pete."

Mickey, Goofy and Captain Doberman got into their airplanes and waved goodbye to Dr. Future.

"Well, I found out what made that car fly," said Mickey to Captain Doberman, when they had landed, "but I still feel kind of let down."

"Let down!" said the captain, surprised. "Why, you got Dr. Future's invention away from Pete and kept Sky Island from falling. I'd be pretty proud, if I were you!"

"Gosh! Thanks, Captain," said Mickey, feeling better.

"You know," said Captain Doberman thoughtfully, "no one would ever believe the things we've seen these last few days."

"You're right," said Mickey. "Goofy doesn't even believe it, and he was there!"

"Let's pretend we never saw Dr. Future's flying car, or his island," said the captain, holding out his hand to shake on it.

"Flying car? What flying car?" asked Mickey, winking. The two shook hands and laughed.